Paula Metcalf

Macmillan Children's Books

For my little sister, Jessie

First published 2008 by Macmillan Children's Books
a division of Macmillan Publishers Limited
20 New Wharf Road, London N1 9RR
Basingstoke and Oxford
Associated companies throughout the world
www.panmacmillan.com

ISBN: 978-1-4050-5126-2 (HB)
ISBN: 978-0-230-01784-9 (PB)

1 3 5 7 9 8 6 4 2

A CIP catalogue record for this book is available from the British Library.

Printed in Belgium

Shirley and Doris were so excited that they woke up very early . . . before the birds, even before the day!

It was Shirley's birthday!

"Happy birthday to me,
Happy birthday to me,
Happy birthday dear Shirley,
Happy birthday to me," sang Shirley.

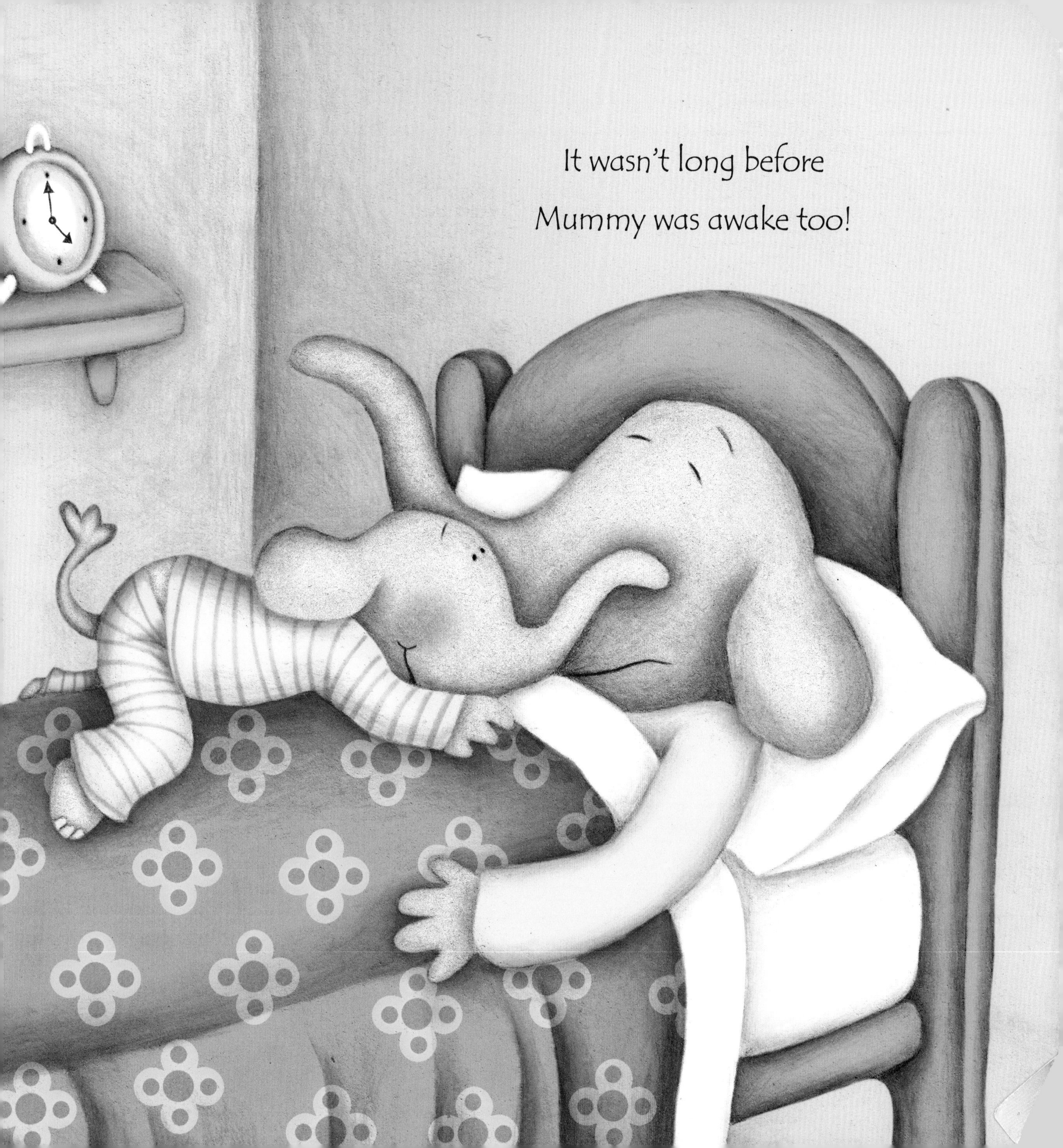

It wasn't long before
Mummy was awake too!

Shirley and Doris spent the morning
getting ready for Shirley's party.

Shirley put on her brand new party dress.

Luckily, Doris fitted into Shirley's old one.

When the party guests arrived they all brought . . .

"PRESENTS!" squealed Doris.

But none of the presents were for Doris.

"Those chocolate toffees look really yummy!" said Doris, hopefully.

"That's because they ARE yummy," said Shirley, "and they are all MINE."

Everyone played Pass the Parcel.

"DORIS! You're not allowed to hold onto the parcel unless the music stops!" said Shirley. "That's why it's called PASS the Parcel."

Then the music stopped.

"DORIS! You're only supposed to take off ONE layer!" said Shirley.

Next they played Musical Chairs.

But the first time that the music stopped . . .

"DORIS IS OUT!" everybody shouted.

It wasn't much fun being the only one out.

So, the next time the music stopped . . .

"SHIRLEY'S OUT TOO!" shouted Doris.

"Right!" said Shirley. "I know a good game. Let's play Hunt the Doris, where Doris goes a long way away and hides."

"HOORAY!" squealed Doris, and she ran off.

Doris was gone for a long time . . .

But she came back – just in time for tea!

"Now, Doris," said Mummy. "It's SHIRLEY'S birthday, so you know who has to blow out the candles, don't you?"

But Doris didn't answer.

"It's MY birthday and they are MY candles!" said Shirley.

She took a deep breath and leaned forward. Then . . .

Shirley blew out the candles all by herself!

"Happy Birthday!" everyone shouted.

"See, Doris! You CAN be a good girl, can't you?" said Mummy.

But Doris didn't answer.

Actually, she COULDN'T answer . . .

"Hmm," thought Doris, "chocolate toffees are sticky

– but just as yummy as I thought!"